BABY BLUE HIPPO

www.idapearson.com
ida.pearson@btinternet.com

BABY BLUE HIPPO

Ida Pearson

First published in Great Britain in 2014

Ida Pearson
Boston
Lincolnshire
ida.pearson@btinternet.com

A catalogue record for this book is available from the British Library.

ISBN 978-0-9555435-2-4

Contents

Family Day Out

Baby Blue Hippo was playing on the sands with his mummy, daddy, sister and brother. They were having lots of fun.

'Please! Can we go and play in the sea?'

Asked Baby Blue Hippo to his mummy?

'What a good idea' said mummy, 'but I think we will go for an ice cream first'.

'Woo! Yes please,' said Baby Blue Hippo.

And, off the family went to get their ice creams.

They found a nice place to eat their ice cream, in the gardens near the rose bushes. The scent from the roses wafted up their noses.

'What a lovely smell,' said mummy, as she watched the roses swaying, with the warm gentle breeze.

'I think we should go to the zoo before we go in the sea,' said daddy.

Baby Blue Hippo agreed, along with his brother and sister.

With the mention of the zoo, Baby Blue Hippo quickly ate up his ice cream, making rather large licks but making sure, he didn't drop any, as he loved his ice creams.

'Ta rare!' said Baby Blue Hippo, 'finished my ice cream.'

The rest of the family were still enjoying theirs.

'Okay,' said mummy 'almost finished,' as she put the last little bit of cone into her mouth.

'Now that was lovely,' she said.

The rest of the family agreed as they pulled themselves up from the grass and made their way to the zoo.

There were lots to see at the zoo and Baby Blue Hippo went to talk to the monkeys.

The rest of the family watched the lions eating their dinner.

Time passed by quickly and it wasn't long before they had been around the whole of the zoo.

'Right,' said daddy, 'the sea it is.'

They all raced back to the sands, trotted down to the sea, into it, and started to swim.

There were some very big waves, which Baby Blue Hippo didn't like very much, he kept well away from them. The rest of the family loved them and waved to Baby Blue Hippo as the waves covered them all up. Baby Blue Hippo waved back, laughing at their game.

Then along came a huge wave. Baby Blue Hippo tried to warn the family but they couldn't hear him.

The huge wave washed over them. Baby Blue Hippo watched in terror. As the wave disappeared, he couldn't see any of his family.

He waited and waited, then along came another wave. Baby Blue Hippo looked on in anticipation.

Then he could see all of his family laughing and waving to Baby Blue Hippo. Once again, he waved back but then he noticed all of his family at the top of the wave, carried away out to sea. All that Baby Blue Hippo could do was watch.

'Ow no!' Said Baby Blue Hippo, in aghast. Then he noticed all of his family waving, he waved back as they all disappeared into the distance, going into another country.

Baby Blue Hippo made his way out of the sea onto the sand. He felt so saddened on knowing that his family had gone to live somewhere else and didn't really know what he should do.

In Another Village

Pink Hippo had been working hard all day making her pretty pink cottage all bright and shiny. She was going away on holiday for a long weekend to her Grandma and Grandpa's home. She could hardly wait for the time to come, when she could set off.

Before that time came, Pink Hippo had to pack her case.

As she did so in the evening, she listened to her music, leaving off the packing for a few minutes to have a dance.

Then she continued with her packing, singing rather loudly to the music.

By the time that she had done all her packing and had a nice long bath, it was almost time for the early night that she had promised herself. She wanted to set off bright and early in the morning.

Pink Hippo was awakened by her alarm. She

quickly climbed out of bed and started to get ready. She had made herself a big breakfast, a bowl of grass and vegetables. She had a long walk ahead of her; she wanted to make sure that she had eaten a good breakfast.

The sun was shining brightly; even though it was early in the morning, it was very warm.

Pink Hippo strapped her case to her back and started out on her long walk, making sure that the door of her pink cottage was locked securely, before she started the long walk.

It wasn't long before it was midday.

Pink Hippo wanted to get to grandpa and grandma's house before teatime.

She decided to stop on the side of the road and have a break, eating her lunch and then off she trotted again, down the road.

It was almost teatime, just as Pink Hippo had planned; she arrived at grandpa and grandma's house.

Grandma was very busy in the garden collecting all the different vegetables for their tea. When she stood up, after bending down, picking the carrots, she noticed Pink Hippo walking through the gate.

Grandma was so pleased to see Pink Hippo. She threw down the carrots and trotted over to great her.

Pink Hippo was pleased to see grandma too.

They both sat on the grass, talking, while Pink Hippo had a nice long rest, before making their way inside for their tea as grandpa had arrived home.

After they had eaten all their tea, they all sat and chatted until it was time for bed.

Pink Hippo said goodnight to Lopsy the cat and Harvey the dog before making her way up to bed.

A Big Surprise

Baby Blue Hippo seemed to have walked such a long way.

When it was almost dark, he made himself a bed, down the dyke bank, in the hay that was there. He felt very sad and started to cry as he missed his family but soon fell fast asleep.

When it was light, he awoke full of sadness and started to cry again.

In the meantime, Pink Hippo, grandma and grandpa were eating their breakfast.

'I know,' said grandma 'let's go for a nice walk as the sun is shining lovely.'

'That would be nice,' Pink Hippo replied.
Grandpa had already made his plans for the day so Pink Hippo and grandma went without him.

The two set off for their walk along the long grass path, joining them was Lopsy the cat and Harvey the dog.

They had walked quite a distance when Pink Hippo could hear a whimpering. She realised that it was coming from the bottom of the dyke. She made her way down the bank, while grandma, Lopsy and Harvey stayed at the top and waited.

Pink Hippo noticed a pile of hay and realised that the sound was coming from there. She gently moved away the hay to find a very tiny Baby Blue Hippo. She lowered herself to the same height as Baby Blue Hippo but he shot up out of the grass and ran further down the bank.

Pink Hippo realised that Baby Blue Hippo was afraid so didn't chase after him but made her way back to the top of the bank to join the others.

They didn't really know what to do but thought it best to leave things for now and come back another time, making their way back to grandma's home.

All that they talked about that day was the Baby Blue Hippo but they knew that there was nothing that they could do about him so left things well alone.

The day was soon over and all three made their way to bed while Harvey and Lopsy slept in their room.

Before long, it became very dark and it was time for Lopsy to go hunting.

She made her way out of the cat flap and raced down the long grass path to where they found Baby Blue Hippo that same day.

She softly made her way down the bank to the big heap of hay. 'Please talk to me,' said Lopsy to Baby Blue Hippo, who was buried deep in the hay once again. 'I will not hurt you, I only want to help you,' Lopsy continued.

Baby Blue Hippo listened to the words of Lopsy and decided to crawl out of the hay.

'I've lost all my family,' said Baby Blue Hippo. 'I'm so sad.'

Lopsy listened intently and knew that she had to think of something quickly, to cheer Baby Blue Hippo up.

'I know,' said Lopsy, 'come with me and help me with my hunting'.

Baby Blue Hippo followed Lopsy along the bottom of the dyke bank.

After they had gone a little way, Lopsy asked Baby Blue Hippo to lay very low, half way up the bank. Lopsy lay by the side of him. They were both very still and quiet, and then they heard a squeak and a rustle in the grass and up popped a little mouse. Lopsy pounced near to the mouse but the little mouse ran so quickly to the bottom of the dyke and continued to run as fast as his little legs would carry him.

Lopsy knew that he was far too fast for her so she gave up the chase.

Although Lopsy did like hunting, she was getting a bit fed up by now. 'What shall we do now,' said Lopsy.

'I know,' said Baby Blue Hippo 'let's go for a swim.'

Lopsy didn't think that a good idea at all as she didn't like the water but as Baby Blue Hippo had been so patient while Lopsy did her hunting, she said. 'Well! You go and I will sit on the bank and watch you and take a rest.'

With all the chasing she had done, Lopsy was beginning to feel rather tired.

'Okay,' said Baby Blue Hippo. 'I'm looking forward to my swim.'

The two went further along the dyke to where the water was quite deep. Baby Blue Hippo jumped into the water making a big splash.

'This is great fun,' he said, swimming his way further along the dyke.

He continued with his swimming, backward and forwards, while Lopsy lay on the bank and watched.

By now it was almost morning and Lopsy could see the light peeping through, as Baby Blue Hippo swam passed Lopsy, she shouted to him. 'It's almost time to leave.'

Baby Blue Hippo climbed out of the water, up the bank to where Lopsy sat. 'But! I've nowhere to go,' said Baby Blue Hippo.

'Oh yes you have,' Lopsy replied. 'You are coming home with me.'

'Really,' Baby Blue Hippo replied, 'won't your family mind?'

'Not in the least,' said Lopsy, 'they are very nice.'

Baby Blue Hippo was really pleased that he had somewhere to go, and off the two of them went, making their way to Lopsy's home.

When they arrived in the drive, Baby Blue Hippo heard a 'woof, woof.'

'Oh no!' Said Baby Blue Hippo, 'I didn't realise you had a guard dog.'

'That's not a guard dog,' replied Lopsy. 'It's just Harvey, who likes people to think that he is an aggressive guard dog but he is a big softy really.'

What a relief that was to Baby Blue Hippo.

Lopsy climbed in through the cat flap.

'I can't get through there,' said Baby Blue

Hippo.

'That's okay,' said Lopsy, 'grandpa will be up shortly to let Harvey out for his morning walk, and you can come through the door then.'

Grandpa left the door open as he stepped outside with Harvey.

When the two was out of site, Baby Blue Hippo came from behind the shed and ran inside, through the door. He went into the room and lay on the mat and within seconds he had fallen fast asleep.

Baby Blue Hippo jumped out of his sleep as he heard voices.

Pink Hippo shouted. 'Grandma come and look who's here.'

Grandma raced in the room and was more than surprised at seeing Baby Blue Hippo. 'I have a strong feeling that Lopsy had something to do with this when she went out hunting last night.'

Pink Hippo agreed.

They all had a lovely day together, chatting on the big lawn, eating vegetables and grass. Baby Blue Hippo played in the grass with Lopsy and Harvey, they had such a good time playing chase me, round the big lawn.

Baby Blue Hippo had forgotten all about his sadness. He couldn't get over how he had met such a nice, happy family and hoped that he would be able to stay there. He knew his family would be so pleased for him.

The day went by so quickly, it was bedtime before they knew it. Grandma gave Baby Blue Hippo a bed that belonged to Lopsy. He climbed into it and although he was a bit big for it, it was nice and comfy.

As grandma, grandpa and Pink Hippo climbed the stairs to their bed, grandma said, 'Well! I've a very busy day tomorrow.'

'What are you going to do?' Asked Pink Hippo.

'Make the spare bedroom up for Baby Blue Hippo as now he will be living with us, he will need a room of his own to sleep in,' replied grandma.

'I will help too,' said Pink Hippo.

They were very excited at the thought and Baby Blue Hippo having heard the conversation was more than happy that he had found a very nice family to live with once again. Although he would never forget his other family that he knew, he would be very happy where he was and hoped that one day he would meet up with his other family to introduce them to the nice family that he had found.